# Evie's Magic Bracelet

**Read more in the Evie's Magic Bracelet series!**

# Evie's Magic Bracelet

## The Sprites' Den

# JESSICA ENNIS-HILL
### and Elen Caldecott

## Illustrated by
## Erica-Jane Waters

Hodder
Children's
Books

HODDER CHILDREN'S BOOKS

First published in Great Britain in 2017 by Hodder and Stoughton

3 5 7 9 10 8 6 4

A CIP catalogue record for this book
is available from the British Library.

ISBN 978 1 444 94209 5

Printed and bound in Great Britain
by Clays Ltd, Elcograf S.p.A.

The paper and board used in this book
are made from wood from responsible sources

Hodder Children's Books
An imprint of
Hachette Children's Group
Part of Hodder and Stoughton
Carmelite House
50 Victoria Embankment
London EC4Y 0DZ

An Hachette UK Company
www.hachette.co.uk

www.hachettechildrens.co.uk

To Grandad Rod and
Grandma Margaret,
whose garden was a
magical place x
– J.E-H.

To Laura, best
studio pal. – E.C.

# Chapter 1

Evie Hall was thinking about magic. She had once had a very interesting meeting with a unicorn that meant now she was able to see the glittering gold sparks of magic. Evie was *also* sitting at the breakfast table eating breakfast. As she shovelled cornflakes on to her spoon, she imagined that the golden flakes were golden discs of magical light floating in the milk.

'Evie,' Mum said, 'stop daydreaming and get eating! I have to be on the ward a bit early today so chop-chop!'

Evie chop-chopped. She shoved a spoonful into her mouth.

'Good girl,' Mum said with a grin.

Evie smiled too – Mum didn't know that magic wasn't just a daydream, it was real. And sometimes there was magic right here in number 6 Javelin Street.

Just then, the doorbell rang.

'That will be the postman,' Mum said. She put down her mug of tea and stood up.

Lily, Evie's little sister, leapt out of her

chair too. 'Presents for me! Presents for me!' she yelled. Tomorrow was Lily's birthday and she had talked about nothing but presents and parties all week.

Lily followed Mum out of the room in the same eager, wiggly-waggy-tailed way that Myla the family Labrador followed Lily.

Evie chewed her cereal thoughtfully. Sometimes she got very, very interesting presents too. Sometimes her Grandma Iris sent magic bracelets which gave her three days of fun and adventure. She'd talked to animals and made toys come to life and all sorts. But Lily was probably right, it was most likely a birthday present for tomorrow.

'Evie!' Mum shouted from the hallway.

'Parcel for you.'

What?

Hurray!

Evie wolfed down the last few mouthfuls and barrelled out into the hall. Mum stood by the open door in the warm sunshine, still talking to the postie. She held a beautifully wrapped parcel in her hand – wrapping that Evie recognised. It was from Grandma Iris!

'That looks exciting,' Mum said. 'Is Grandma Iris sending you one of her lovely treats again?'

'I hope so!' Evie said. Mum had no idea just how lovely the gifts from Grandma Iris could be.

'Lucky thing,' Mum said with a smile.

Lily sat hunched on the bottom stair;
she scowled like an angry troll guarding
a bridge.

Narky because the present wasn't for her,
no doubt.

Evie ignored Lily completely, and took
the parcel from Mum. A present from
Grandma Iris was worth a happy dance
at the very least. It might be a bracelet!
She jumped, whirled and shimmied in the
middle of the hall.

'Careful, you'll have someone's eye out!'
Mum said.

Fair enough. Evie ducked into the good
front room. She shut the door behind her.
Lily mustn't watch.

The whole room felt as though it crackled
with electric excitement as she sat on the
sofa and carefully untied the ribbons. Would
it be a new magic bracelet? Please, please let
it be. There was a neat little box under the
paper. She lifted the lid …

… Yes!

There was a beautiful bracelet inside.

It was strung with a row of tiny, identical coral-coloured beads. She took it out of the box and put it on her wrist. Golden sparkles immediately bloomed above her head – magic appearing because she was so happy.

'Thank you, Grandma Iris!' she told the dancing sparkles.

She knew that when she twisted the bracelet three times around her wrist, then magic would flow out of it and cause all kinds of things to happen. Each bracelet gave her a different power, while it lasted.

She looked inside the box. Grandma Iris usually sent a note to explain the bracelet's power – although the notes were usually annoyingly tricky to understand. They never came with an instruction manual, more's the pity.

There. She found the small piece of card, with Grandma Iris' poem written on it.

Just be careful what you think,
A giant truck, a kitchen sink,
Might just be an idle thought,
Until the moment you get caught!

Great. She had no idea what Grandma Iris meant with her riddle, but it sounded like trouble. 'Be careful', 'get caught'. It would be so much easier if Grandma Iris told her exactly what to avoid.

Still. Evie had a feeling that whatever it meant, she was going to find out sooner rather than later.

She smoothed out the ribbons and wrapping paper, folding them neatly. She would add them to her box of art materials later. She didn't have school today, it was the summer holidays, but she tucked her bracelet under her sleeve anyway – she didn't want Lily asking for a turn wearing it. Lily would find a way to break it, or messy it, or smear it with jam fingers.

Lily was still outside, sitting on the stairs,

though Mum had gone back to the table. She still had a troll-face as she glared at the spot where the postie had stood.

'Don't worry,' Evie said. 'You'll get your presents tomorrow.'

Lily didn't reply, she stuck out her bottom lip like a tiny shelf on her face.

'Evie! Lily! Please come and clear your breakfast things,' Mum called.

'Are you coming?' Evie asked Lily.

Lily didn't move a muscle.

'Suit yourself.'

Evie was too happy about her new bracelet to worry about Lily's moods. What sort of new magic could it do? What adventures might she have? And, importantly, what was she supposed to be careful of?

The living room was empty, except for Myla the dog, who was curled up asleep below the table. Mum had cleared the cereal boxes from the table and taken them through to the kitchen. Only the dirty bowls and glasses were left.

She was alone.

This was a perfect chance to see what the bracelet could do.

Evie slipped her left hand under her right sleeve and twisted the bracelet, once, twice, three times ...

Straight away a ribbon of gold light twisted around her arm, snaking its way towards her fingers.

'Evie!' Mum called from the kitchen.
'Bring the dirty glasses through, please.'

Evie only half-heard. She was too busy
watching the magic twirl and twist.

'Evie! Juice glasses!' Mum shouted,
running hot water into the sink.

Evie thought about a glass of juice.

*Ping!*

A glass of juice popped into the air in front of her.

What?

It hovered there, in midair, for a micro-second. The glass reflected the gold light on her wrist, the orange juice sloshed slightly inside.

Then, as if the glass realised that there was absolutely nothing at all holding it up, it fell to the ground.

It landed with a smash on the floor. Juice spilled everywhere, splattering the carpet, the table legs and the chairs. The glass shattered into fragments, jagged edges glistened.

Myla, under the table, leapt in fright.

Evie gasped.

What had just happened?

'Oh, Evie!' Mum was in the room, drawn by the noise. 'Did the glass slip? Mind your feet. Don't move, I'll get a dustpan. Myla, out of here, come on, in the garden. I don't want you cutting your paws.'

Mum and Myla bustled out of the room together.

Evie was left standing beside the broken glass, which had just appeared the moment she had idly thought of it.

She remembered Grandma Iris' poem: 'just be careful what you think'. The thing she'd thought about had just appeared in the middle of the living room, conjured by magic. It *was* a really good job she hadn't

thought of a giant truck. The house would
have been squished. Grandma Iris was right,
she had to be careful.

# Chapter 2

Mum sent Myla out into the sunshiny garden, then came back into the room with a dustpan and brush.

'I'll do it,' Evie said. 'I'm sorry I dropped it.' She didn't want Mum to pick up the glass in case it vanished as soon as it was touched, or turned into jelly or something equally deeply suspicious – it *was* made by magic, after all.

'No. Thank you, Evie, but I don't want you cutting yourself either. I guess I'm just not going to be getting to work early today after all. It was probably too much to ask for a simple morning.'

'Sorry,' Evie said again.

'Oh, don't worry. I know it was an accident. Worse things happen at sea.' Mum dropped pieces of glass on to the dustpan with gentle clinks.

'What happened?' Lily's voice came from the doorway. 'I heard a totally massive smash!' She sounded a bit more cheerful after the disappointment of the parcel –

she was probably pleased that Evie was in the doghouse.

'Just an accident,' Mum said brightly.

Evie kept a watchful eye on the broken pieces – were they showing any signs of jelly-ness? No. They behaved like perfectly ordinary glass. Phew.

In a few moments, all the big pieces were collected and Mum had run a mini-hoover over the carpet to lift any tiny shards.

'All done,' she said. 'Now, I really do have to get to work. You're off next door to spend the day with Nana Em and Grandpa, isn't that nice? Shoes on now, girls, quick as you can.'

There was the usual scramble to find Lily's

shoes, with lots of where-did-you-last-see-
them, while Evie tugged on her trainers.
A day with Nana Em and Grandpa was
brilliant – they might go to the park or the
city farm, or maybe they'd take a picnic out
to the moor and watch birds sail through
white fluffy cloud.

But she hoped that whatever they did with
the day, there would be a chance to use her
new bracelet too. Perhaps she could conjure
up some nice cakes for tea, or maybe a pogo
stick? She'd always wanted to try bouncing
on one of those.

She should absolutely tell her friends
Isabelle and Ryan about the bracelet too.
They'd been a huge part of all her magical

adventures and she didn't want them to miss out on this one. Isabelle would have a list as long as a giraffe's scarf of things she'd want to conjure – a pony, or a swimming pool, or a Ferris wheel were all probably going to be near the top of her list. Things that were going to be pretty tricky to hide from Nana Em.

It was a short hop next door – through the kitchen, out of the gate at the end of the garden, left along the ginnel that ran behind the houses, then through Nana Em's garden gate. Mum waved them goodbye from the kitchen door.

Lily ran ahead – she always wanted to be first at everything, even getting through the garden gate. She was gone. Evie dawdled in the warmth of the sun, smelling the scent of roses and wisteria trailing over the fence. Their big paddling pool stood empty in the middle of the grass, the orange hose coiled beside it ready. Mum said they could fill it at the weekend. Evie smiled. She loved the summer holidays.

'Nana! Grandpa!' Lily's voice floated back to Evie. Then, 'Oh! Oh no!' Lily cried out. There was shock and horror in her voice.

Evie picked up the pace, trotting down the ginnel. What was wrong? What had upset Lily?

It was obvious the first second she walked through Nana Em's gate.

Grandpa's beautiful garden, that he loved and cared for, was a total mess, an awful shambles. Huge chunks of lawn had been ripped up, flowers had been snipped from their stalks, petals fallen to the ground; twigs had rained down on to the heads of the garden gnomes and the wishing well Grandpa had made from tiny bricks was splattered with mud.

23

And sitting in the middle of all the mess
was a very muddy Myla.

'Oh no,' Lily said, 'Myla, you didn't?'

'Is that you, girls?' The shout came from
inside the house. Grandpa.

Evie looked at his garden. She looked at
Myla, who wagged her tail gently. Myla

had mud on her paws and face. Was there anything Evie could do? Anything she might conjure to stop the disaster that was about to happen, as soon as Grandpa saw?

She couldn't think of a single thing.

Grandpa had reached the back door. His normally rosy face turned pale as he looked at the wreckage.

Myla gave a soft woof. A torn leaf dropped from her nose.

'Oh, no. Bad dog,' Grandpa said. 'Bad girl.'

Myla stood slowly. She tucked her tail tightly between her legs, dropped her ears and hung her head.

'You're in disgrace,' Grandpa added.

'No!' Lily cried. 'Myla wouldn't have ruined your garden. She loves chasing the bees and sniffing all the flowers.'

Grandpa spread his hands, the palms calloused from shovelling and hoeing. 'Who did this, then? It wasn't you girls, was it?'

'Of course not,' Evie said hotly.

'Well, there you go, then. I'm afraid she's caught red-handed. Red-pawed. She's got to go straight home to bed to think about what she's done. No treats at ours today, Myla. Go on, go home.'

With her head still bowed, Myla waddled towards the back gate. She whined gently as she walked past Evie, but she did as she was told and headed home.

'Poor Myla,' Evie whispered.

But Grandpa had very good hearing. 'Give over. Poor Myla? What about me, eh? What about my garden? Poor Myla, my foot. She's made a right old mess.'

Evie didn't say anything, but she didn't believe it for one minute. Myla would never do such a thing.

But who had? And why?

There was a mystery here, and she was going to be the one to solve it.

# Chapter 3

The first thing she had to do was to call
Isabelle and Ryan – she was going to
need back-up.

Grandpa gave Lily a wire broom from
his shed and they were working together to
sweep the worst of the mud splatters off
the stepping stone path.

Evie slipped past them, into the house. Grandpa wouldn't want guests when his garden was in such a mess, but she needed the others to come quickly.

The kitchen was quiet. Sunlight dappled the warm wood of the units. Huge basil and chilli plants on the windowsill made the room smell delicious. Where was Nana Em? Evie stood still, straining to hear, but there was no sound.

The coast was clear.

She crept through the dining room and into the hall. At the bottom of the stairs was a little table, with the phone on it.

Evie knew Isabelle's mobile number off by heart. She lifted the receiver and dialled quickly. Isabelle answered on the first ring.

'Hello, Evie's nana,' Isabelle said.

'Hello. It's me,' Evie hissed. 'Come over
quick and get Ryan. There's magic and
a mystery.'

'You had me at hello,' Isabelle said. 'What
sort of magic? What does it do? What's the
mystery?'

'Isabelle …'

'OK, OK. Tell me when we get there.
We'll be two shakes of a lamb's tail. Don't
do anything without us. I want to see
everything.'

'Evie?' Nana Em said behind her.

Evie slammed down the phone.

'What's the matter, petal? Who was that

on the phone?' Nana Em asked.

Busted.

'Is it OK if Isabelle comes over? Even though the garden is a mess. And Grandpa is worried. And Myla is in disgrace. And Ryan too. Not in disgrace, I mean, can Ryan come over?' Evie splurged in a rapid rush. She was no good at thinking of excuses under pressure – that was Isabelle's speciality.

Nana Em was frowning. Would she say no?

'The garden is a mess? Is Grandpa all right? I'd better go and check.'

Nana Em bustled down the hall like a hen clucking after chicks.

Evie grinned. She'd definitely asked permission to have friends over. And Nana Em hadn't said no.

She opened the front door and kept a watchful eye on the street beyond the tiny strip of front garden.

It wasn't long before she saw Isabelle marching with purpose down the road, her dark hair swishing from side to side. Ryan was more relaxed, strolling along behind her.

Isabelle grinned as she stomped up the path. 'Magic and mystery? Tell us everything. Go.'

Evie filled them in on everything that had happened that morning.

'So,' Ryan checked, 'you think Myla is innocent, but she's been found guilty on the most circumstantial of evidence?'

'Circum-what-now?' Evie asked.

'He's been watching too many cop shows,' Isabelle added.

'It means there's no real proof,' Ryan explained.

'That's exactly it! There's no proof. And I can't believe that Myla would do it. We have to clear her name,' Evie agreed.

'Let's get out there, and let's get to work,' Ryan said.

'Definitely too much telly,' Isabelle said.

Grandpa hadn't done a bad job of tidying, but the garden still looked sad and sorry for itself. He had filled a green sack with broken branches and snapped stems. Nana Em had collected the flower heads to put in vases of water. Lily was stomping on the divots, pushing the chunks of lawn back in place. Around them, the plants, shrubs and trees drooped limply.

'I think that's all we can do for now,' Grandpa said.

'Time for a nice restoring cup of tea,'

Nana Em said, patting his arm.

The grown-ups went inside.

'Time for us to look for clues,' Ryan said.

Lily's head shot up, her foot froze above a stray clump of grass. 'Clues? Clues of what?' she asked.

'Nothing!' Evie said. 'Nothing at all. You go and see if Grandpa's all right. OK?'

Lily's bottom lip wobbled. 'Don't want to. I want to stay with you.'

'Well, you can't.' There was no way Evie could use magic in front of Lily – and magic might come in very handy on their search. 'Go on. Go inside.'

'Won't.'

'Lily. We don't want you. Go and play

with Grandpa or Nana Em,' Evie said slowly.

Lily's bottom lip stopped wobbling and started quivering, trembling and twitching until she burst into noisy tears. She turned on her heel and rushed towards the kitchen. She gave the back door a good, hard slam on the way in.

Evie felt her face redden. She hadn't meant to upset Lily, just get rid of her for a bit.

'She'll be OK,' Isabelle said patting her arm. 'Come on, let's search for clues.'

'We need magnifying glasses!' Ryan said.

'We don't have any,' Isabelle replied.

'Not yet. Evie, do you think you could manage?'

Ooh, conjuring. Magnifying glasses would be a big help on the search. Could she do it? The glass of orange juice that morning had just been an accident. She could give it a try though. The note from Grandma Iris had said she just had to think of the object she wanted to conjure.

Evie thought magnifying glasses. She

reached for the bracelet on her wrist and twisted it three times. All the time she pictured round frames, glass bulging in the lens, and dark, delicate handles. Gold light shimmered and sparkled in a magical mist. She closed her eyes and tried her hardest to see the object in her imagination.

*Ping!*

*Ping!*

*Ping!*

Her eyes snapped open.

Three perfect magnifying glasses had appeared in front of them. 'Catch!' Evie said.

They all reached out and caught the handles, before the glasses fell to the ground.

'Cool!' Isabelle whispered. 'It worked. So, we do our investigation, and clear Myla's name, and then we can concentrate on conjuring a whole new summer wardrobe for us all. Orange is really in this year.'

Evie held her magnifying glass up to her eye. Isabelle's head swelled to four times its normal size through the lens. 'Isabelle, think clues, not clothes.'

Isabelle nodded seriously.

Ryan bent down, holding his glass before him. He checked the blades of grass, the clipped flower stalks, the smeared roof of the wishing well.

'Hey!' he said. 'Look at this.'

Evie peered at the side of the well, where

Ryan was pointing. She held her glass carefully in front of her.

There, in the middle of the drying mud, was an unmistakable footprint. It was small, the shape of a teardrop with one tiny toe on the end. She had a very good idea of who might leave a print like that.

Evie was sure it belonged to a mischievous little sprite!

# Chapter 4

'Sprites!' Evie hissed.

'Where?' Isabelle spun in a circle, spying as hard as she could with her magnifying glass. Her eye bulged menacingly.

They had met mean little sprites on an earlier magical adventure. They were tricksy creatures who flew around causing mischief

and mayhem wherever they went – and
delighted in doing so.

'Where are they?' Isabelle demanded.

'That's what we have to find out,' Evie
said. 'And then we can clear Myla's name.
It must have been the sprites who ruined
Grandpa's garden.'

'Maybe Myla was trying to chase them away,' Ryan added. 'That's how she got so muddy.'

Evie's heart felt as though it had swelled to twice its normal size. She'd known Myla would never have damaged Grandpa's garden deliberately and she was right – Myla had been trying to defend it!

'Right,' she said crossly. 'I want to find those sprites and give them a piece of my mind.'

The hunt was on. They had to examine every inch of the garden from the stoop by the back door to the gate at the end of the garden. No stone would be left unturned. No leaf left unshaken. No twig left unstirred. This was serious.

Isabelle obviously agreed. 'We're going to need to be properly equipped for the job,' she said firmly. 'Boiler suits for everyone! I don't want to get my new dress mucky.'

Boiler suits? Like the huge overalls Dad wore to work? No thanks! Evie folded her arms.

'Don't look like that!' Isabelle said to her. 'You've got magic powers to make anything appear! We have to use it. And what better way to make sure I don't get into trouble with Mum when I get home for splattering myself with mud?'

Ryan laughed. 'I don't think you've ever once had a telling-off. Your mum and dad think you're perfect.'

'I am perfect,' Isabelle said with a wide grin. 'Perfectly clean, that is. And I want to stay that way. If you would be so kind, madam?' Isabelle sank into a deep curtsy in front of Evie, with her arms spread wide like a ballerina's. She wobbled a bit, but managed to get down low without keeling over.

Evie felt herself grin. It might be a good idea to protect their clothes. And she could do with the magical practice.

Fine. Boiler suits it was.

Evie took a deep breath and twisted her bracelet three times. In the bushes she could hear the trilled song of a robin, and an aeroplane flew over leaving snowy trails in the sky.

*Boiler suit. Boiler suit. Boiler suit*, she thought, over and over, as the magical golden light streamed around her wrist. The light sped up, a glittering swirl of motion. She felt the fizz of magic in the air.

The robin shot up out of the bush with a sudden, harassed tweet.

*Ping.*

*Ping.*

*Ping.*

Boiled sweets burst like fireworks above their heads and tumbled down on to the grass. Dozens of red, orange, green and purple sweets in wrappers lay at their feet. Oh. The robin had distracted her and they'd ended up with boiled sweets

instead. Evie felt her cheeks flush red with
embarrassment.

'Wow!' Ryan said. 'It's not boiler suits,
but I for one am pretty pleased about that.'
He gave her a wink and she felt a little bit
better. He picked up the nearest sweet,

unwrapped it, and popped it into his mouth. 'Hmm. Straw'ree flavour.'

Isabelle picked up a green one and licked it. 'Lime, my favourite!'

Evie sighed. She'd thought she might be getting better at controlling the magic – she had made the magnifying glasses appear, after all. But she'd definitely made a mistake this time.

Quite a tasty mistake, though. She unwrapped an orange one and sucked on it thoughtfully. She'd better gather up the goodies in case Nana Em came out and thought they'd raided a sweet shop!

They made short work of collecting the sweets in an empty plant pot.

'No more sweets until we've found the sprites,' Evie said. 'We need to earn our reward.'

'What about my dress?' Isabelle asked.

'Fine, I'll try again. But don't blame me if you end up with boiled spuds. OK?' Evie said.

She concentrated as hard as she could this time. She closed her eyes, so she wouldn't be distracted by Isabelle or Ryan watching eagerly, or a startled robin. She tried to block out the sounds of the neighbourhood – cars out in the front street, a radio blaring from a garden further along, pigeons having a noisy disagreement up on the roofs somewhere.

She just tried to picture the perfect boiler suit – navy blue arms and legs, a bright gold zip running up the front.

*Boiler suit*, she thought, and reached for her bracelet. *Boiler suit*.

*Ping.*

*Ping.*

*Ping.*

She opened her eyes. Lying on the grass were three perfect, navy blue suits.

'Woo-hoo!' Isabelle clapped her hands together in delight. 'That's awesome!'

'Well done, Evie,' Ryan added softly.

She'd done it. Evie pulled one of the suits over her legs and slipped in her arms. It was exactly the right size. It had worked.

The others were ready in a flash.

And then, they set about hunting for the naughty sprites.

# Chapter
# 5

Once they were all zipped into their suits
and they held up their magnifying glasses,
they looked like proper investigators. Now
they just had to follow the clues to find the
sprites' den.

'Where did it go from the wishing well?'
Evie asked, as she examined the tiny

footprint. Sprites had wings, so it might have flown anywhere. She looked up. High above, the green branches of a birch tree spread over the garden, their leaves rustling in the breeze.

'There!' Ryan said. 'Look, the leaves have been torn and broken on that branch.'

With her magnifying glass, Evie could see what he meant. It looked as though something with tiny hands had ripped the leaves. So, the sprite had gone from the well to the tree. Then where?

'Here!' Isabelle called eagerly. 'There are more torn leaves.' She stood beside a bush that drooped cones of purple flowers. Evie wasn't sure what it was called, but she knew

Grandpa had planted it for the butterflies. Isabelle pointed at a patch of green leaves which had been raked to ribbons.

Isabelle drew back the branch and peered into the shadows of the bush.

'Ow!' She stepped back quickly. There was a splat of mud on her arm. She wiped at it quickly. 'I got hit,' she said, outraged. 'Someone threw mud at me.'

'Sprites,' Evie gasped. 'You found them.'

'Listen!' Ryan said, holding up his palm.

They could hear high-pitched squeals. The sprites were horrified to have been discovered. Evie could hear them whispering.

'The Big Ones can see us!'

'No they can't!'

'It's looking right at me.'

'Liar!'

'Am not a liar!'

She heard scuffles and a few yelps of pain, before something fell with a squelch into mud. Then, there were giggles, like a mouse chuckling at a joke. A mean joke.

Evie lifted a stick from the ground and used it to push back the branch, careful to keep her distance. The giggling got louder and she saw a flash of blue as a sprite darted across the shadows. They were definitely hiding here.

Evie leaned in to get a better look.

'Watch out!' Ryan called.

But it was too late – *thud!* – a ball of mud hit her right on the chest. *Thud, thud, thud*. Three more thrown. They hit her, *ow, ow, ow,* on the shoulder, on the knee, on the cheek.

Then, small stones and twigs flew out of the shadows, bouncing and stinging as they rained on the three friends.

'Get back!' Isabelle yelled.

They stumbled away from the bush, and ducked behind the wishing well. There wasn't enough room for all three of them, so they had to squish close together.

Evie looked at the others. There was mud on Ryan's face and twigs in Isabelle's hair. They both looked battered and bruised. She probably looked exactly the same way herself.

'We need shields,' Ryan said. 'Something to keep the muck off us.'

He was right. They couldn't get closer without some protection. She looked around the garden. There was nothing big enough, just a watering can and a trowel.

'Conjure something,' Isabelle said.

Could she?

She'd have to try.

What they needed was a good, sturdy umbrella, like the one Dad took on the rare Saturdays when he was able to go and play golf with his friends.

The howls of glee from within the bush grew louder. She knew there were at least two sprites, and she wondered if there might be more.

*Umbrella*, she reminded herself.

A big, sturdy one. Right. She was on it.

The high-pitched giggles sounded cruel.

She closed her eyes and put her hand to her bracelet. She felt a warm current of gold magic against her skin. *Great big golfing umbrella*, she thought, trying to ignore the sound of the sprites. *A ginormous one, big enough for three.*

The sprites laughed at her, and she could hear them whispering too.

*Ping!*

She opened her eyes.

On the ground beside the wishing well lay a paper cocktail umbrella. The kind of thing Nana Em put on top of ice cream sundaes for a special treat.

Isabelle patted her arm. 'Don't worry,' she said. 'At least you tried.'

Suddenly, the branches parted and two blue sprites rushed out, whipping up into

the air. Their fine wings fluttered, lifting them upwards. Their hands were loaded with gravel and they giggled excitedly. The biggest one hurled a small stone – it pinged off the wishing well. A second sprite launched his attack. Evie felt a stone whizz past her ear.

'Retreat!' she yelled. 'Everyone inside!'

They raced indoors as fast as they could, with stones showering down around them. They closed the back door firmly behind them and stood on the kitchen tiles, dusting themselves down. Through the window, they could see the two sprites fly a victory lap around the garden, kicking their long legs and clapping their hands, before diving back into their den.

'We're a right mess!' Isabelle said indignantly. She peeled off her boiler suit and dumped it on a chair. Mud fell on to the tiles in clumps.

'We need to get rid of the sprites, but also clear Myla's name,' Evie said.

'Grown-ups can't see magic,' Ryan added. It was true. There was no point at all in telling Grandpa about the sprites – he wouldn't be able to see them. How on earth could they fix this?

Just then Nana Em came into the kitchen. She eyed the drying mud.

'Have you been trying to clear up the garden?' she asked.

Evie gave a shrug that might mean yes,
and it might mean no. They sort-of had been
trying to clear up!

'Well, you can be useful inside too,' Nana
Em said. 'I'll need help blowing up balloons
for Lily's birthday party soon.'

Oh no. They had loads more important

things to do than get ready for a silly
birthday party – the sprites were still out
there, giggling like they ruled the garden!
Evie crossed her arms and felt her jaw set.

'Don't look like that,' Nana Em said.
'Lily needs your help to make sure she has a
lovely birthday.'

Evie thought about the magic that had
gone wrong outside, the tiny umbrella
instead of the proper protection they
needed. She had a responsibility to put
things right for Grandpa, and Myla, and
she had blown it.

'I don't want to think about stupid Lily's
stupid birthday. I don't care about her
party,' Evie snapped.

There was a gasp from the kitchen
doorway.

Evie looked over, just in time to see Lily –
who had heard every word.

# Chapter 6

Lily had tears in her eyes, as she stood at the edge of the kitchen. Her face looked red and blotchy. 'Well,' she said angrily, 'I don't care about you either. I don't even want to have a party.'

She turned on her heel and marched down the hallway.

'Evie, that was a mean thing to say!' Nana Em said sternly.

They all heard the front door open – and slam closed.

'Lily's gone out into the street,' Nana Em said, the worry clear in her voice.

Evie glanced at Ryan and Isabelle. They looked worried too. 'I'll go after her,' Evie said. She raced down the hallway and out of the front door. The front garden was small, but Grandpa crammed in as many flowers and plants as he could. The curling, creeping green fronds and bursts of petals hid the street from view. Evie trotted down the path to the pavement.

There, she saw Lily, with Myla clipped

on to her lead. Lily had gone to fetch Myla
and now they were both headed who-knew-
where. Lily looked very little beside the big
Labrador.

'Lily!' Evie cried.

Lily completely ignored her, as though Evie were a lamp-post, or a wheelie bin.

'Lily! You're not supposed to be out in the street by yourself,' Evie shouted. Playing out the back was fine, but Mum would have kittens if she knew Lily was out by the road.

'I'm not by myself,' Lily snapped over her shoulder, 'I'm with Myla.'

Lily's hair bounced as she stomped away – every curl on her head seemed indignant. Myla plodded at her side.

They stopped at the bus stop at the end of the street. Lily sat on the bench under the shelter. Myla sat patiently at her feet. They both watched the road. There was no sign of a bus in the traffic that crawled past slowly.

Evie joined Lily on the bench. They sat in silence.

Evie didn't know what to say.

From the way that Lily was twisting Myla's lead around her wrist, Evie could tell how cross she was.

Myla gave Evie a short lick on her knee. At least someone was pleased to see her.

'Where are you going?' Evie asked finally.

'To London,' Lily replied. 'Or New York.'

'Have you got the bus fare?' Evie asked.

Lily didn't reply. But the lead whipped around faster and faster.

'Mum will be worried if you're not here when she gets back from work,' Evie tried again.

'What do you care? You don't care about anyone but yourself.'

'That's not true!' It wasn't true at all! Evie was always helping Ryan and Isabelle. And she always offered in class when Miss Williams wanted a volunteer. And she always did everything Mum and Dad asked her to do.

'It is true,' Lily snapped. She glared at the cars as they drew level with the bus stop. Her eyes still glistened with tears.

'You do whatever you want with your friends and you never want to spend any time with me, or Myla. You never even gave her a fuss this morning when she got into trouble. All you wanted was to call Isabelle and Ryan and have them come over to play.'

Myla panted in a patch of sunshine that spread across the shelter. Evie's hand reached out to rub the soft fur on the top of Myla's head. 'I had things I needed to do,' she told Lily.

'You've always got things to do. You never have time for us any more.' Lily didn't sound angry now, she sounded sad.

Was it true? Evie felt like she played with Lily and Myla and Luna the cat, all the time. But maybe she had been so swept up by learning about magic with Isabelle and Ryan that she hadn't had time for much else lately.

Myla nudged Evie's leg with the wet tip of
her nose.

Evie bit her lip. 'Wait here,' she told Lily,
'and whatever you do, don't get on a bus.'

Evie ducked behind the back of the bus
shelter. She would conjure something! She'd
make something so wonderful, so amazing,
that Lily would cheer right up, and forget
the horrible thing she'd heard Evie say about
her birthday.

Her birthday! That was it. She'd conjure a
birthday cake, with candles and everything,
and give it to Lily now.

All she needed was for the magic to
go right.

She checked the street. Over in the far

distance, one of the neighbours was busy clipping their hedge. Another was washing their car in front of their house. Would anyone notice a bit of magic being done on Javelin Street? Nana Em said the neighbours could be right curtain-twitchers sometimes, which didn't sound like a good thing to be.

Still. If it was what Lily needed to cheer her up, then Evie would have to take that chance.

She grabbed hold of her bracelet and thought, as hard as she could, *cake, cake, cake,* then she twisted it three times.

*Ping!*

Right in front of her appeared a teensy, tiny, weenie cupcake. She reached out and

caught it before it fell to the ground. It was
miniature, but it looked like a birthday
cake, with frosted pink stripes and scalloped
white icing.

It was much, much smaller than she'd
been going for – her spells were still going

more wrong than right – but she hoped it would be enough to cheer up Lily.

# Chapter 7

Evie carried her mini little cake back around the bus shelter to where Lily was still sitting. Myla's nose shot up into the air and she sniffed appreciatively – cake was one of her top favourites, along with biscuits, buns, bread, batter and leftovers.

'Sorry, Myla, it's not for you,' Evie said.

Lily was slouched on the bench, her shoulders drooped like a thirsty plant. At the sight of the pretty little cake, she smiled and her head rose expectantly. 'Is that for me?' she asked.

'Of course. It's to say, well, just for you really. To cheer you up.'

Lily was still looking at her – waiting for something else.

Evie wasn't sure what. 'You should eat it and come back inside.'

'Is it a bribe?' Lily asked. Grandpa sometimes gave them treats after they helped around the house. Dad would frown and say in a specially stern voice that the treats were bribes. It was clear Dad didn't approve.

'It's not a bribe. It's a cake. Do you want it or not?' Evie sighed. Lily was even being difficult about cake!

Lily reached out and took it. She ate slowly, chewing every delicious mouthful – without offering even the smallest nibble to Evie.

'I'm going to come indoors,' Lily said, once she'd wiped the crumbs away with the back of her sleeve, 'but I'm not doing it because of you. I'm doing it because Myla has already been in trouble today and I don't want her to get shouted at again. And Myla has forgotten her bus fare.'

Lily stood and looped Myla's lead around her wrist. Myla thumped her tail, hoping for a walk. But they were only going back to the house.

Evie trailed behind, feeling a little bit uncomfortable. She'd done a nice thing for Lily – given her a cake a day early! – but Lily didn't seem happy. And it hadn't made Evie feel better either. She had a sneaking,

stealthy feeling in her tummy that what
Lily had wanted more than a cake was
an apology.

Lily dropped Myla back at their house,
then went and rang Nana Em's doorbell.
It was Isabelle who answered. 'You're back!'
she said in delight, looking right at Evie
and ignoring Lily completely. 'Good. We
need you right away. Not only is there the
*thing* about the *thing* to talk about, but also
your nana won't stop going on about the
other *thing*.'

Isabelle was being deliberately mysterious.
That was just like her – if there was a drama
to be made out of something then she'd be

the one directing the script.

But it was the wrong moment to be dramatic with Lily.

Lily turned to Evie, her face pink with rage again. 'Fine,' she said, 'fine, you keep your secrets with your *friends*. See if I care. I don't even want to know what you're up to.' She turned away. 'I. Couldn't. Care. Less.' With every word, she stomped up the staircase to Nana Em's bedroom, where Evie was sure she would run and hide and sulk. Perhaps even cry a little bit.

Evie dithered at the bottom of the stairs. She owed Lily a proper sorry. But then, Isabelle needed her too. What should she do?

Isabelle decided for her. She slipped her arm through Evie's and dragged her away from the bright sunlight in the doorway, through the hall to the kitchen.

Ryan was sitting at the neat little foldaway table that Nana Em used to give the girls their tea. He had a glass of lemonade in front of him and a smile on his face. 'Your nana is lovely,' he said.

'There are sprites on the warpath and you think this is a good time to take a break?' Isabelle said scornfully.

'Nana Em made me!' Ryan said. 'One minute I was a boy in charge of my own destiny. The next, I'm sitting here with a glass of pop.'

'Nana Em is a force to be reckoned with,' Evie agreed. 'Where is she now?'

Ryan pointed up towards the strip light. 'Upstairs. She went to see how your grandpa is doing. She said we had to help with balloons. Is Lily all right?'

Evie felt a twist of guilt. She really hadn't been very nice to Lily. 'She's just mithering,' she said with a flick of her hand.

'We've got no time for balloons,' Isabelle said. 'What about the sprites? They're still out there.' She went to the kitchen window and stood on tiptoes so she could peer over the sink. The garden looked quiet enough, branches swayed in the breeze and the robin bobbed his way along the lawn. There was no sign of the sprites.

'You're right,' Evie said. 'If the sprites stay they'll find a way to ruin Lily's party anyway. It's just the sort of thing they'd love to do. We have to get them out of the garden.'

She heard footsteps, coming slowly down the hall and towards the kitchen. Nana Em stepped into the room. Normally her coral pink lips were set in a smile, but not now. Now, she looked as angry as a bull with homework.

'Evie Hall,' Nana Em said sternly. 'Why is Lily so upset?'

Evie shrugged. She felt her cheeks flame.

'Did you say sorry for the mean thing you said?' Nana Em put her hands on her hips.

She'd given Lily a present and tried to cheer her up!

But, as Evie looked at the floor as though she was suddenly very interested in Nana Em's trainers, she knew she hadn't done the thing that really mattered.

'Oh Evie,' Nana Em said. 'I think maybe it's time that your friends went home. You,

young lady, have to help with the party
plans, but, most of all, you have to make
things right with Lily.'

# Chapter 8

Isabelle hastily kicked some of the mud from view. 'We can help with Lily's party too!' she said. Evie knew that she didn't want to get sent home while the sprites were still about.

Nana Em didn't reply straight away. Isabelle put on her widest, most winning smile.

Ryan stood and walked to the sink. He rinsed his glass and then dried it with a tea towel. 'Which cupboard should I put this in, Nana Em?' he asked. His smile was as wide and sweet as Isabelle's.

Nana Em rolled her eyes. She wasn't fooled by their helpful act for one tiny second, but she also liked Ryan and Isabelle. 'Fine,' she said, 'fine, you can stay. But you really do have to help. I want to see the pass-the-parcel wrapped, and the pin-the-football-on-Bill-Foulke made. I want to see more balloons than I've had hot dinners. Is that clear?'

Isabelle and Ryan nodded eagerly.

Nana Em pulled Evie closer, into the

soft cloud of her perfume. Her ash-gold
hair tickled Evie's skin as she leaned in to
whisper. 'I want to see you put things right
with Lily,' she said.

Evie would. She really would.

But right now the sprites were more
important. So she didn't say anything at all.

Nana Em patted her shoulder, clearly
confident that her point had been made.

'Right. Your grandpa fancies a cup of tea, and who am I to stand between a man and his brew? You lot, go into the living room and make a start.'

Evie, Isabelle and Ryan were forced to leave the kitchen – and the sprites – under Nana Em's watchful stare.

Nana Em's living room was full of photos of family. Evie could see gentle wisps of gold magic floating around the silver photo frames. When people were happy, magic was never far away. As well as the photos, Nana Em had some china shepherdesses arranged on the mantelpiece and a vase of flowers fresh from the garden. She'd put all of the party things on the low coffee table.

Isabelle took out a balloon and gave it a stretch. Then she put it to her lips and blew. The balloon flapped a bit, but didn't inflate in the slightest. Isabelle tried again, her cheeks puffed out like a goldfish. Nothing. Her face went redder and redder, tomato bright in seconds.

'This one's broken!' she said.

'You're just not doing it right,' Ryan said. He grabbed a balloon and gave the biggest, longest puff he could manage. The red plastic made a farty noise and stayed flat as a pancake under a truck.

Evie started to giggle.

Both her pals huffed and puffed like the wolf in the fairy story. They looked – and

97

sounded – so silly that she couldn't help it – she just had to laugh. Soon she was whooping, clutching her sides until her belly ached. Gold swirls of magic danced about her in delight.

Isabelle threw down the balloon in a strop. 'If you think it's so funny, you have a turn!' she said.

'Even better,' Ryan added, handing her a balloon, 'use magic to blow them up.'

Evie stopped laughing. 'I can't,' she said, 'I don't know how. I can't just imagine air inside the balloons and make it appear.'

'How do you know when you haven't even tried?' Isabelle asked.

It was a good point. Mum and Dad were

always saying she should just try her best. She definitely hadn't tried her best when she hadn't even tried at all!

Evie closed her eyes and imagined a bunch of balloons, jewel-coloured, in green and red and purple, dancing at the end of strings. She held them there clearly, in her imagination, then reached for her bracelet.

*Ping!*

'Oh,' Isabelle gasped.

Evie opened her eyes. A dozen perfect balloons bobbed in the air, all trailing string. One floated up to the ceiling and bounced gently against the artex. She reached out and grabbed the bunch before they all followed suit.

'Perfect!' Ryan said. 'Your Nana Em will be really pleased.'

'If only I could solve the sprite problem with balloons,' Evie laughed, delighted that the magic had worked so well.

Ryan froze. His eyes widened, his head jerked up. It was clear that he had had an idea.

'Balloons,' he said slowly. 'Water balloons.'

What? Ryan wasn't making any sense.

He bounced up and down on the tips of his toes in excitement. 'Water balloons! Remember the last time we had to deal with sprites? You were able to chase them away with water. They hate water. What if we head out into the garden with water balloons?'

Gold sparks of magic fizzed above him – his enthusiasm was clear.

Evie thought ... and found herself growing more and more excited too.

It was a great plan. Sprites would do anything to get away from water.

If the three of them went out and hurled water balloons at the den then the sprites would make a dash for it, she was sure.

All she needed was to conjure enough water balloons to do the job.

Her confidence faltered for a second. She had conjured a silly little umbrella instead of anything that was good for protecting them, and a tiny little cake when she was going for a show-stopper. But then, the balloons she'd just conjured for the party were absolutely perfect.

'Do you think I can do it?' she asked.

Isabelle nodded. 'Of course we do!' she said warmly.

'No question,' Ryan added.

Well, she thought, if her friends believed in her, then she would have to at least try.

# Chapter 9

Evie tied the balloon strings to the back of a chair to stop them all bobbing away. Then, she put her mind to some serious conjuring. She would need not just the balloons, but the water inside them. If she got it wrong, she might totally soak Nana Em's settee, or flood the living room – or even make the whole house sopping!

'You can do it,' Ryan said softly.

Evie closed her eyes. She imaged a perfectly round water balloon, full-to-sloshing with water. In her mind it was baby pink, and just the right size to fit in her palm.

She held her right hand out. She didn't want the balloon to fall and smash in the way the glass of orange juice had done that morning. She reached for the bracelet and turned it three times, all the while thinking *water balloon.*

*Ping!*

She felt it first, heavy and squishy in her palm. She dared to open her eyes, just a peek.

There, in her hand, was exactly the thing she'd imagined.

'Yay!' Isabelle cried. 'Now make more.'

Ryan grabbed the wicker trug from the grate and lifted the logs out of it. He took the first balloon and rested it, careful not to pop it, in the basket.

Evie imagined water balloons again and again and again. Each time she did it, Ryan was able to add a new one to their collection. Soon they had a tower of missiles, ready to be thrown.

'Let's go,' Evie said, when there was room for no more.

She checked the hall. No one was about, so they headed back to the kitchen, where they pulled on their boiler suits. Then they stepped into the garden.

The scene was still and quiet. Evie could hear traffic in the distance, and the tinkling song of an ice cream van, but there was no sign of the sprites.

'Keep low,' she warned the others, 'don't let them know we're here.'

They crept closer to the bushes at the back of the garden ... when Isabelle trod on a stray twig. It snapped in two with a loud *crack*.

Immediately they heard a rustle in the dark branches. A scattering of leaves rained to the ground. Then telltale high-pitched giggles told them they'd been spotted.

A blue sprite whizzed from the shadows. Another flitted up into the air. They

whipped from branch to branch, like streaks
of blue lightning.

'Silly kiddies back again!' one sprite yelled.

'Where's their mud gone?' the other
replied.

'Here it is!' the first one said, before
launching a ball of mud in their direction.

'Aim missiles!' Ryan yelled as a clump
of mud splatted near his feet. The girls
didn't need a second invitation. Evie held
a water balloon in the cup of her palm,
then launched it hard and fast, towards
the enemies. It missed! It burst in a shower
of drips on a flagstone. Isabelle launched
another. And another. Ryan too. The two
sprites swerved right and left, up and down,

avoiding the strikes like fighter planes dodging attack.

Then the sprites returned fire, swooping to the ground and grabbing handfuls of dirt and grit. They hurled it at the children. Evie and the others were soon streaked with gunk.

'Hey!' Isabelle yelled at the sprites. 'This is my favourite boiler suit! You won't get away with this.' She grabbed water balloons in both hands, ready to fire.

Evie grabbed two too. Ryan took the last two from the basket. 'On my count!' Evie said. 'One, two, three – NOW!'

All six balloons launched at the same

time. They hurtled towards the two sprites from all directions. There was nowhere for them to duck, dive or dodge. The balloons made contact and immediately exploded, soaking the two sprites from wing tip to toe.

'Aieee!' the smaller sprite yelled.

Evie could see his tiny little eyes shrivel to pinheads. His sharp teeth were bared in a grimace. Water dripped from his wing tips, but it hadn't made him flee – it had just made him very, very angry.

'Uh-oh,' she said softly.

He grabbed the other sprite and dragged him up to a branch. The two crouched there. Evie could hear frantic whispers. What were they scheming?

It didn't take long to find out.

The two sprites clapped their hands – gleeful at whatever they had decided. Then they launched themselves in whirling circles, getting tighter and tighter, corkscrewing down to their target – Grandpa's compost bin.

It was the place where all the food scraps and peelings went. Friendly insects chewed the food down to rich, dark earth, ready to feed the garden. But that meant the newest layers were full of rotting potato skins and woodlice.

'Uh-oh,' Evie said again. 'I think we should take cover.'

'What?' Isabelle asked.

'Take cover!' Evie yelled. They all ducked behind the wishing well, as best they could. But there wasn't really enough room for all of them.

One of the sprites kicked the lid off the compost. A few flies swooped up from the mix. The sweet smell of rotting veg floated towards them.

The sprites dived down. Then swept back up with armfuls of brown, gloopy mulch.

'Eww!' Isabelle moaned.

'Get ready to stink!' a sprite yelled.

'No!' Isabelle covered her head with her arms.

Just then, the garden gate burst open. Myla charged through ... carrying the end

114

of Mum's garden hose in her mouth!

'Myla, come!' Evie called.

The dog trotted closer. The sprites buzzed nearer, struggling with the huge bundles.

'We need to turn on the water!' Ryan yelled. He ran from the cover of the well, past Myla, following the trail of the hose.

The sprites were right overhead. Dark drips splatted on the wishing well roof.

Myla dropped the hose at Evie's feet. Evie grabbed it and pointed it straight at the sprites. Would Ryan reach the tap in time? Were they about to be stink-bombed from a great height?

'Close your mouth,' a sprite warned with an evil chuckle.

As he opened his arms wide, letting go of the rotting veg, Evie felt the hose in her hands tremble. Then a huge jet of water shot out, pushing aside the falling veg and hitting the laughing sprite right in the middle of his chest!

He shot straight up into the sky, shrieking. Evie swivelled the hose until it hit the second sprite too. He was drenched in seconds and went fleeing after his friend. They rose like arrows into the air, getting smaller and smaller until they were just specks. Finally, they were gone.

Myla licked Evie's hand. She patted the top of the dog's head firmly. 'What a clever girl,' she said. Myla seemed to grin.

Then she padded happily away, through the garden gate, to her own house next door. She passed Ryan, who was on his way back.

'Did we win?' Ryan asked.

Evie looked at her friends. Ryan's normally gelled hair was mussed up and flecked with dirt. Isabelle had a muddy streak down one side of her face. But they were both smiling.

'We won!' Evie said.

They'd done it, they'd chased away the sprites and made the garden safe. Isabelle slowly picked up the basket and collected the tattered pieces of burst balloon.

Evie eased aside the branches of the bush and looked at the sprites' den. It was a dark hole in the ground, lined with bits of rubbish they'd pulled in – old crisp packets and damp-looking newspaper mostly.

'What have you found there, pet?' Grandpa's voice said behind her.

She turned. He was walking towards them from the house, cradling a fresh mug of tea and looking more tired than she'd seen him look in a long time.

'I'm not sure,' Evie stammered, not at all certain what she should say. How could she tell Grandpa what had happened?

'Hmm,' Grandpa said, 'it reminds me a bit of a fox hole, though it's not quite right. Could there have been a fox here, do you think? They can do a lot of damage if they put their mind to it.'

Evie held her tongue. She absolutely didn't want to lie to Grandpa, but she also didn't think that it was the best idea to tell him he had a sprite problem in his garden.

'If there were foxes,' Ryan said wording his sentence carefully, 'then maybe they were the ones who ruined the garden, not Myla. Maybe she was the one trying to defend it.'

'Do you think?' Grandpa said thoughtfully. He peered into the bush and dropped down to take a closer look at the den. 'Something with bad habits has definitely been here. Look at all this mess,' he said. 'Aye, lad. Happen you're right. Maybe I was a bit quick to accuse Myla.'

Evie fizzed with golden joy – they really had done it! 'Does that mean Myla's in the clear, Grandpa?' she asked.

Grandpa gave a slow grin. 'I reckon it does. Go and get her, would you? It seems I might owe that dog an apology.'

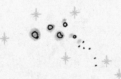

# Chapter 10

Evie wasted no time in fetching Myla. She
found her at home, sitting proudly beside
the back door. She'd helped defeat the sprites
and she knew it.

'Myla!' Evie called. 'Come with me,
there's a good girl.' At the words *good girl*,
Myla bounded to her feet, her tail thumping

from side to side trailing gold glitter – 'good girl' sometimes meant treats.

They both went back to Grandpa's garden, where – sure enough – Grandpa waited for them with a sausage roll he'd snaffled from the fridge. 'It's meant to be for Lily's birthday,' Grandpa whispered to Myla, 'but

Lily wouldn't mind sharing, I'm sure.'

Myla wolfed down the snack and licked her lips. 'Woof!' she said in delighted agreement. Grandpa ruffled the top of her head. 'There'll be more where that came from, I'm sure. Em always cooks too much for Lily's birthday.'

*Lily.*

Evie felt a guilty sort of feeling settle in her tummy. Myla wasn't the only one who was owed an apology. She had made the balloons for Lily's party, like Nana Em had told her to. But, Nana Em had also told her to make things right with Lily and she definitely hadn't done that. Lily still hadn't come downstairs.

Ryan must have seen her frown. 'What's the matter?' he asked. 'Myla's not in trouble any more.'

Evie went to sit on the edge of the wishing well. Isabelle joined her and Ryan sat on the grass at their feet, in a splash of bright sunshine. Grandpa disappeared inside with Myla, who was still hopeful that there were more sausage rolls going spare.

'What's up?' Ryan asked again.

'Lily,' Evie said with a sigh.

The others nodded slowly. They were too good friends not to know what she meant.

'Hey, I've got it!' Isabelle said. 'We can give her a present early, to help cheer her up. We've still got some of the boiled sweets you accidentally made. They're in the flower pot. Give her some goodies, she'll like that.'

Evie thought for a second, but then shook her head. 'That's no use. I gave her a cake, but she just called it a bribe. Sweets would be the same thing.'

'What then?' Ryan asked. 'Is there anything you could conjure that she might like?'

Evie considered. Lily liked lots of different things – a toy or a scooter or some new paints would all make her smile. But Evie knew that none of those things would be quite right. No. What Lily really wanted was a proper apology – and to be invited to join in with them sometimes.

Saying sorry was harder than doing magic.

But she knew it was what she had to do.

'Wait here,' she told the others. She went into the house, and up the stairs. Evie was pretty sure she knew where to find Lily. She'd be in her favourite place in Nana Em's house – inside the fitted wardrobes in Nana Em's bedroom. They ran across one side of the room, with big, white doors with gold trim and gold handles. Evie tapped on the far door and opened it slowly.

Inside was a row of coats: green wool, checked tartan, even one fake fur one that was nice to cuddle. Below that were shoes: high heels and kitten heels, boots and brogues. And beside those, curled up in a corner, sat Lily.

'Budge up,' Evie said.

It was a crush inside the wardrobe together. Something not very soft poked into Evie's side. But it was nice in there too. It smelled of Nana Em's perfume, with shoe polish and wool somewhere beneath the perfume.

Evie ran her fingertips along the hem of the soft fur, stroking it like a cat.

'I'm sorry,' she said finally.

'What for?' Lily demanded.

'I'm sorry for being mean to you and not letting you join in. I shouldn't have. It was wrong.'

Evie thought that Lily wasn't going to reply. Then, Lily leaned across and wrapped her arms around Evie. She buried her face in Evie's shoulder and squeezed tight. 'It's all right,' Lily muttered.

They stayed like that for a while, huddled together in the soft dark. Then, Evie began

to notice that the light wasn't coming from outside in the bedroom, it was coming from the two of them. They were both wrapped in gold magic, like the warm light of a lantern.

Then, Lily bobbed up out of the hug and said, 'Are Ryan and Isabelle still downstairs?'

'Yes, they are.'

'If I ask them to play in the garden, will they want to, do you think?'

'I think they might.'

Lily scrambled over Evie's feet to get out of the wardrobe. 'Then race you downstairs!' Lily cried. 'Last one there is a stink bomb!'

Evie whooped and chased after Lily, both
of them barrelling into each other on
the landing, and bumping each other
on the stairs.

'No pushing!' Nana Em called from
somewhere close by.

'I won! I won!' Lily insisted, giggling in
delight at the bottom of the stairs.

'Perhaps by one tiny centimetre,' Evie
agreed – it was Lily's birthday tomorrow
after all.

Ryan and Isabelle were sitting in the
sunshine in the garden when Evie and Lily
went to join them. They smiled at Lily.

'Tag?' Ryan suggested.

'Haven't we got to wrap the pass-the-parcel, and make a pin-the-football-on-Bill-Foulke?' Isabelle hissed to Evie.

Lily screamed as Ryan lunged to tag her.

'Not just now,' Evie told Isabelle. 'Magic can help with that later. Right now, we've got more important things to do.'

She leapt up, as Lily thundered towards her and the game got properly under way.

# Evie
## and
## friends

# Evie

**Full name:** Evie Hall

**Lives in:** Sheffield

**Family:** Mum, Dad, younger sister Lily

**Pets:** Chocolate Labrador Myla and cat Luna

**Favourite foods:** rice, peas and chicken – lasagna – and chocolate bourbon biscuits!

**Best thing about Evie:** friendly and determined!

# Isabelle

*Full name:* Isabelle Carter

*Lives in:* Sheffield

*Family:* Mum, Dad, older sister Lizzie

*Favourite foods:* sweet treats – and anything spicy!

*Best thing about Isabelle:* she's the life and soul of the party!

# Ryan

*Full name:* Ryan Harris

*Lives in:* Sheffield

*Family:* lives with his mum, visits his dad

*Pets:* would love a dog …

*Favourite foods:* Marmite, chocolate – and anything with pasta!

*Best thing about Ryan:* easy-going, and fun to be with!

# Can you find all the words?

~~BRACELET~~        ~~ISABELLE~~

~~FRIENDS~~         ~~MAGIC~~

~~SPRITE~~          EVIE

RYAN               ~~MYLA~~

~~BIRTHDAY~~        ~~SUMMER~~

| F | X | Z | Z | L | S | B | T | E | S |
| A | R | M | F | U | C | E | Y | L | P |
| V | F | I | M | O | L | T | F | L | R |
| S | E | M | E | E | D | V | Z | E | I |
| X | E | I | C | N | I | E | E | B | T |
| R | R | A | V | E | D | K | N | A | E |
| L | R | D | E | E | M | S | A | S | F |
| B | I | R | T | H | D | A | Y | I | D |
| C | I | G | A | M | L | R | R | Z | A |
| Z | H | O | G | Y | V | T | R | W | P |
| V | K | S | M | W | S | Y | W | O | L |